D0570747

Emma Dodd
PRESENTS

CINDERELEPHANT

ARTHUR A. LEVINE BOOKS
An Imprint of Scholastic Inc.

Once upon a time there was a lonely girl called Cinderelephant.

Cinderelephant lived with her two cousins, who were known as the Warty Sisters. They were horrible, mean, and smelly, and they had no table manners.

They made Cinderelephant do all the cooking and cleaning,
and they **never**, ever said, "Thank you."

Cinderelephant was sad and tired and fed up
with being ignored.

One day, an invitation arrived from the palace. Prince Trunky had decided it was time he found a girlfriend, so King Saggy and Queen Wrinkly had invited **all** the girls in the neighborhood to a ball.

The Warty Sisters were very excited and started to plan what they would wear.

"If they are inviting all the girls," said Cinderelephant, "perhaps that includes me!"

"Of course you won't be going, Cinder-irrelevant!" laughed the Warty Sisters. "Whoever would want to dance with **you**?"

The day of the party arrived, and the Warty Sisters dressed up in their most fashionable clothes.

"Bye-bye, Cinderelephant!" they called as they left the house. "Don't wait up—we're bound to be home very late!"

Poor Cinderelephant sat all alone in the silent house.

A **big** tear rolled down her trunk and plopped onto the floor.

"Hey," squeaked a small voice.
"Watch where you drop those tears! I'm getting soaked!"

Cinderelephant saw a tiny mouse looking up at her crossly.
"I'm sorry," she sniffed, "I'm just feeling sad that I can't go to the party. Excuse me for asking, but who are you?"
"Why, I'm your Furry Godmouse, of course!" he exclaimed.
And with a flick of his magical tail he said . . .

"You shall go to the ball!"

"Wow, you look amazing! Go to the party and enjoy yourself,"
said the Furry Godmouse, "but,

and it's a **big but . . .**

you **must**
be home by midnight."

At the palace,
Prince Trunky was bored.
He didn't want to dance
with any of the girls—he was
worried they might get
squashed! If only he
could find someone a bit
more his type . . .

But wait!
Who was this vision of loveliness
that had just walked in?

"Clear the floor!" bellowed Prince Trunky.

“Wanna dance?”

he asked Cinderelephant, as he swept her off her feet and onto the dance floor.

Prince Trunky
and Cinderelephant danced
together for the rest of
the evening.

"Who is that?"
everybody asked enviously.

"She looks a bit like . . . but no,
it can't be—she looks so good,
and she's such a great mover!"
said the Warty Sisters.

Cinderelephant
had never been so happy.
She didn't notice the
time passing until
suddenly the clock
struck midnight.
"Oops!" she exclaimed.
"I've got to go home!"

As she rushed from the palace,
she dropped one of her
beautiful shoes.

"Wait! What's your name?" Prince Trunky called after her, but Cinderelephant had already gone.

At his feet lay one of Cinderelephant's fabulous shoes.

Then and there, Prince Trunky made a decision
(and Prince Trunky's decisions carry a lot of weight).

Picking up the stiletto, he declared, "I shall find the girl
whose foot fits this shoe—and I shall **marry** her!"

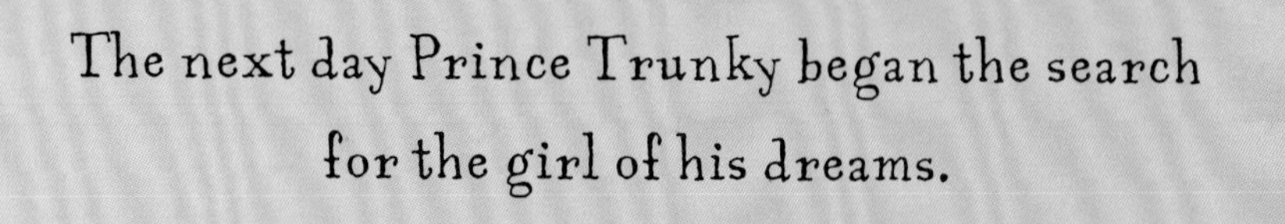

The next day Prince Trunky began the search for the girl of his dreams.

He went from house to house trying the fabulous shoe on every girl's foot.

It fit nobody.

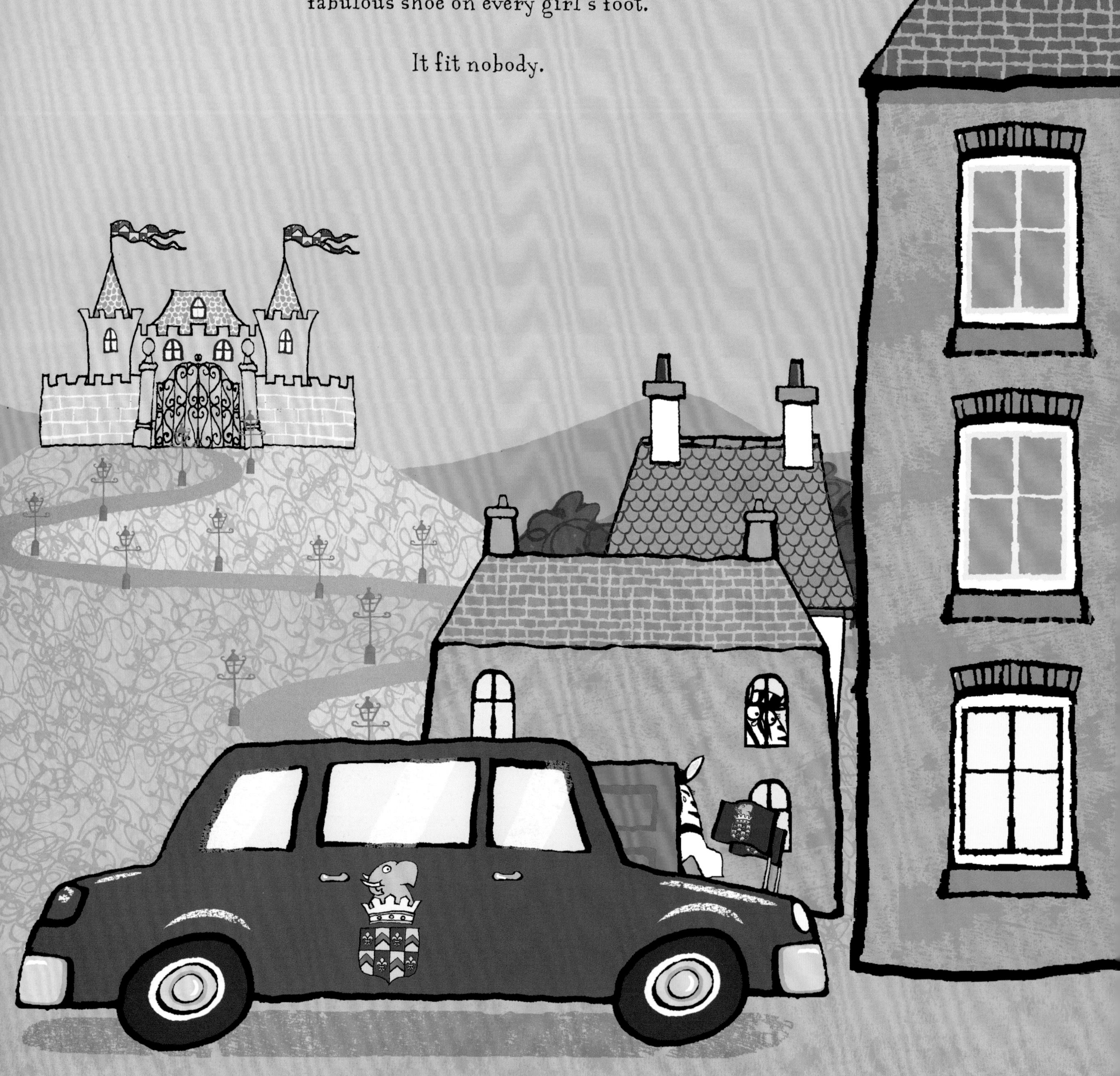

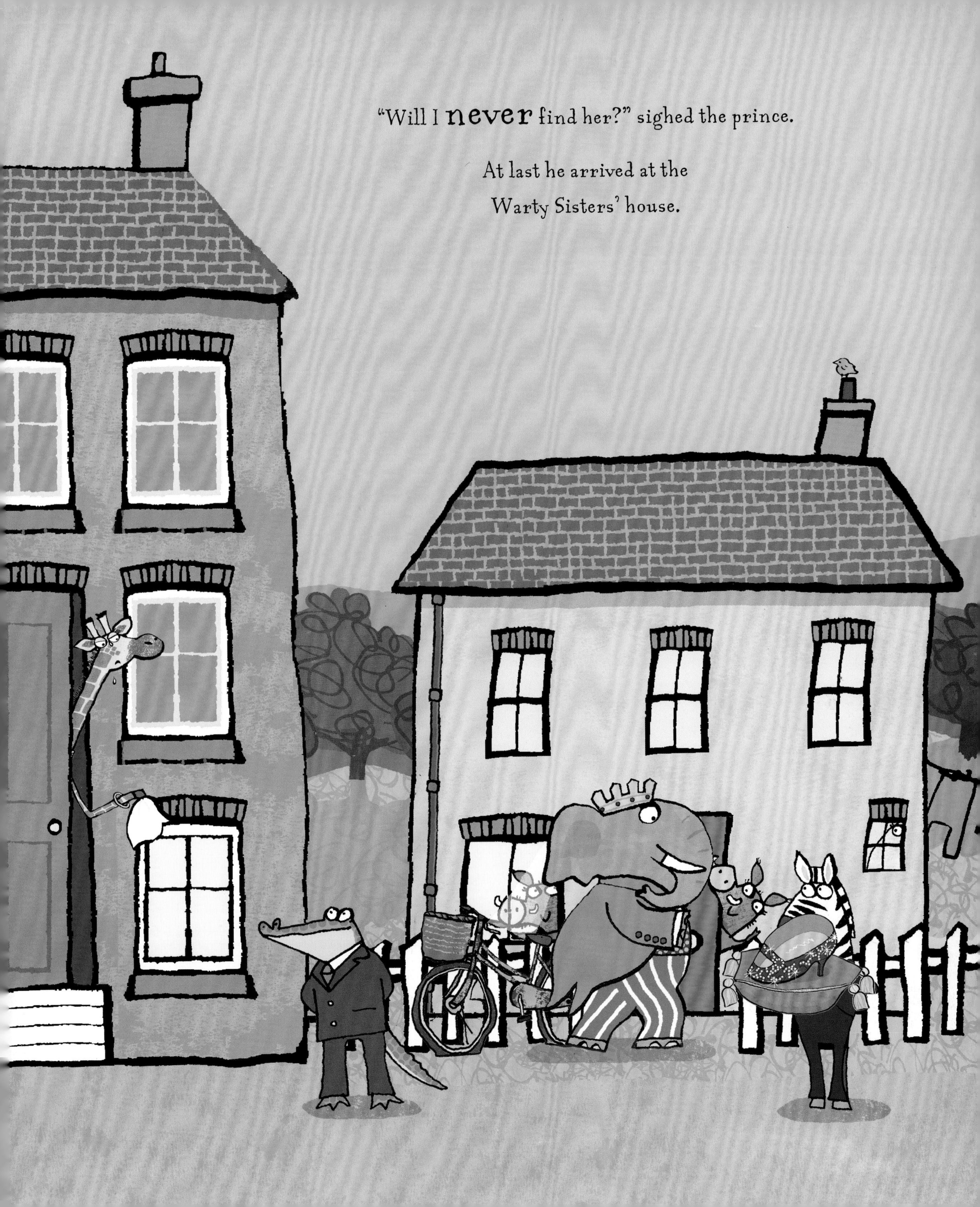

"Will I **never** find her?" sighed the prince.

At last he arrived at the
Warty Sisters' house.

"Give me that shoe," demanded one Warty Sister. "It's bound to fit me!"

But of course her little trotter was

far too small for the gorgeous shoe.

"Let me have a go," said the other sister, snatching it.
"I am Prince Trunky's one true love!"
But of course it did not fit her either.

Sighing quietly to herself, Cinderelephant peeked shyly through a crack in the kitchen door.

But . . . **whoops!**

She accidentally stepped into a bucket,
knocking over the mop, bringing a pile of pots and pans
crashing and clattering down.

"Who is in there?"

asked the prince.
"Oh, nobody important!"
said the Warty Sisters hurriedly.
Taking no notice, Prince Trunky
went to investigate.

"Could it be you?" asked the prince,
slipping the lovely shoe onto
Cinderelephant's foot.
It was a perfect fit.

"You are the one for me!"

cried the prince in delight.

Cinderelephant had never been so
enormously excited in her life.

Cinderelephant and Prince Trunky were married the very next day.

And, of course, they were **hugely** happy ever after.

For Rose and Fay, with love from Emma xx

Library of Congress Cataloging-in-Publication Data
Dodd, Emma, 1969-
Cinderelephant / Emma Dodd. – First American edition. pages cm
At head of title: Emma Dodd presents. • Summary: A lonely elephant mistreated by her warthog cousins charms Prince Trunky with the help of a furry godmouse. •
ISBN 978-0-545-53285-3 (hardcover : alk. paper)
[1. Fairy tales. 2. Folklore.] I. Cinderella. English.
II. Title. • PZ8.D66Ci 2013 • 398.2–dc23 •
[E] • 2012028907

10 9 8 7 6 5 4 3 2 1 13 14 15 16 17

First American edition, October 2013

Printed in China

The art for this book was created digitally.